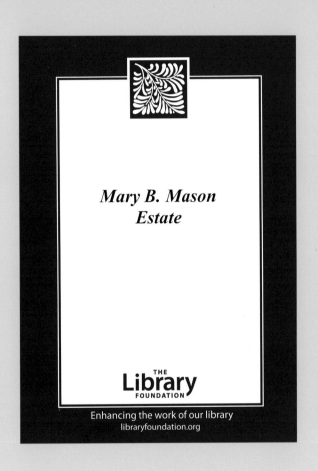

ON GULL BEACH

ON GULL BEACH

BY JANE YOLEN

PICTURES BY BOB MARSTALL

The Cornell Lab
Publishing Group

Designed by Hans Teensma, Impress

Library of Congress Cataloging-in-Publication Data available.

ISBN: 978-1-943645-18-3

Manufactured in China

10 9 8 7 6 5 4 3 2 1

Produced by the
Cornell Lab Publishing Group
120A North Salem Street
Apex, NC 27502

www.CornellLabPG.com

For Jason, Joanne, Caroline, and Amelia, and all the beach walks in their lives.

—J. Y.

For Kristie Miner, a great friend and colleague. Thanks for all of your input on this series of books. Special thanks to Jayden Gulla, the perfect model for this book, to John Polak Photography for photographing the finished art, and to Dennis Nolan for his suggestions and encouragement along the way.

—B. M.

CPSIA TRACKING LABEL INFORMATION
Production Location: Everbest Printing, Guangdong, China
Production Date: 12/15/17
Cohort: Batch No. 80305

By buying products with the FSC label you are supporting the growth of responsible forest management worldwide

As I was walking on Gull Beach,
I saw a starfish within reach.

Set down my pail of sticks and stones,
Of shells and bleached small ends of bones.

But as I bent by wave and spray,
A gull flew down, snatched star away.

I followed quickly on the strand,
My feet left footprints in the sand.

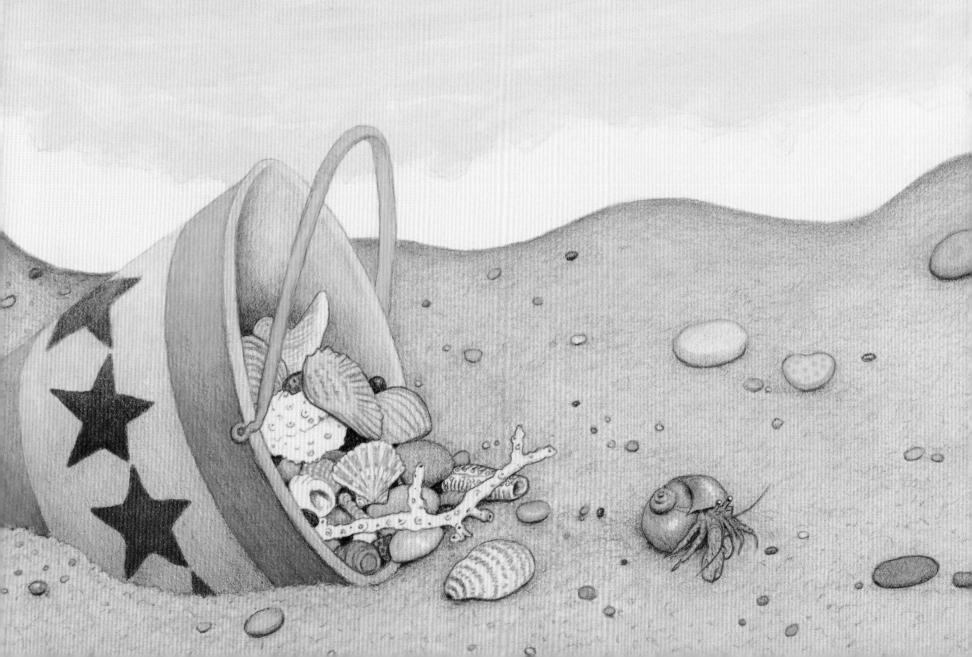

The gull was faster, wing by wing,
And in his mouth, his star plaything.

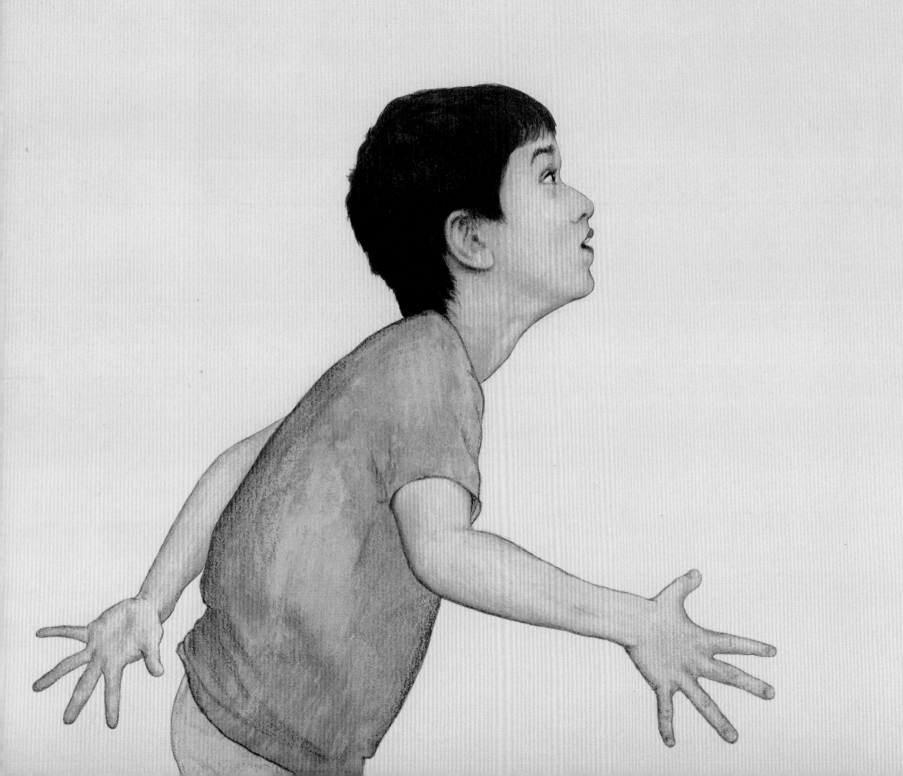

Then as I watched him from afar,
That gull let go—a falling star.

Quickly, I reached single-handed,
To catch the star before it landed.

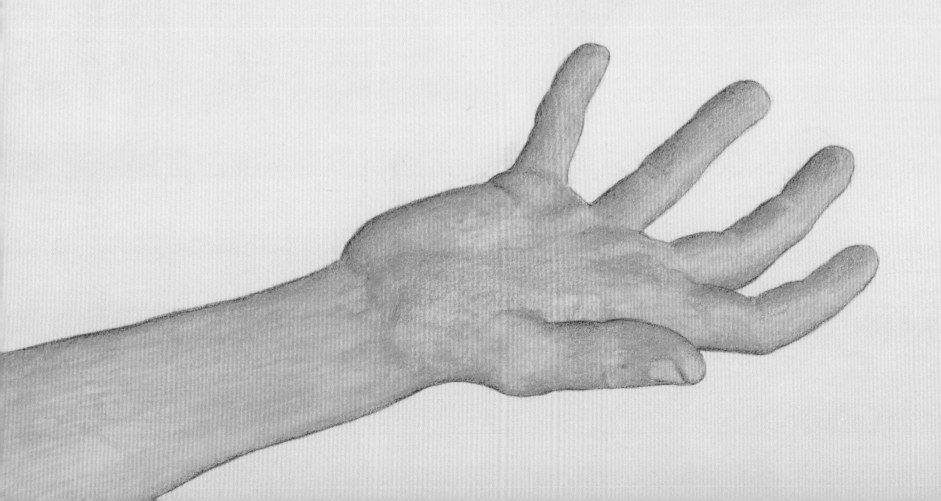

Another gull sliced through the air,
And grabbed the sea star falling there.

But other gulls—all loud and shrill—

Passed the star from bill . . .

. . . to bill.

I raced more swiftly, running after,
Following their gullish laughter.

Ran by rocks and smooth sea glass.
Stumbled over dunes and grass.

Splashed through tidepools at my feet.
Passed by waders, slim and fleet.

Dodged the scurries of small crabs,
Pincers making quick, sharp jabs.

The final gull gave one loud shriek,
And with that, opened up its beak.

The star came shooting down to me.
I reached up for it tenderly.

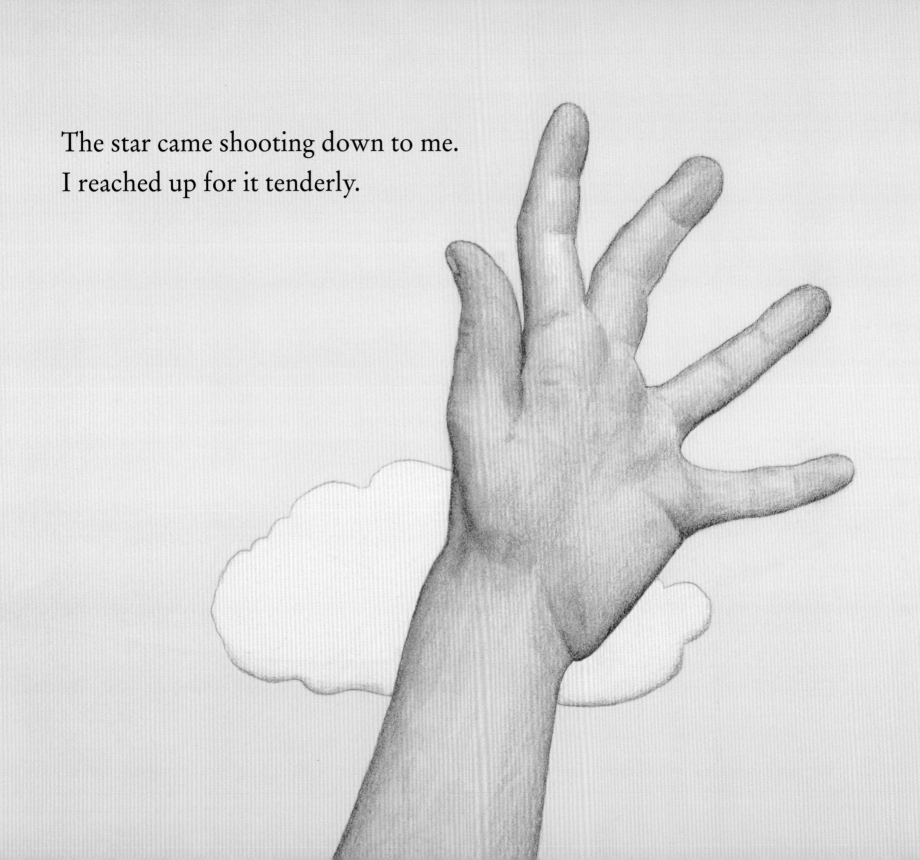

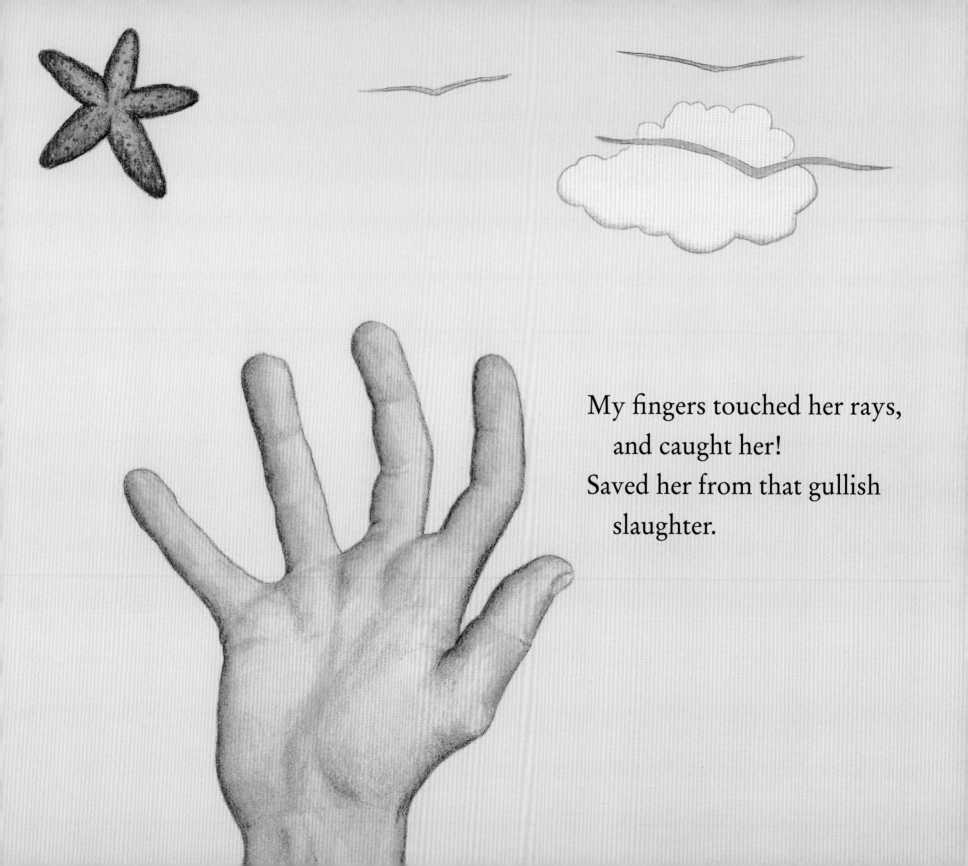

My fingers touched her rays,
and caught her!
Saved her from that gullish
slaughter.

Put her back into the water,
Far out of their reach.

There she sank down in the sea.
Hurrah for starfish!

Huzzah for me!

As I walked home from Gull Beach.

LIFE ON A NEW ENGLAND BEACH

SO MANY GULLS!

The gulls in this book are Herring Gulls, but did you know there are many other kinds of gulls too? There are more than 20 species of gulls in North America alone.

People often call them "seagulls," but they're not always found by the sea. You may find gulls in prairie marshes, along inland lakes, at town dumps, even in the Arctic, and often miles from the ocean. Gulls mostly eat sea stars, fish, crabs, and other animals they find on the beach. They'll also help themselves to your picnic or any leftovers they find in the trash.

Gulls are smart. They recognize individual people and remember them. If gulls think you pose a threat (like getting too close to their nest), they might poop or vomit old fish on you. That is why some gull researchers wear rain gear...even when the sun is shining.

Herring Gull

HERRING GULL BY KEITH PRITCHARD/SHUTTERSTOCK

Listen

How do you know it's a Herring Gull? Look for pink legs, yellow eyes, and a red spot on the lower beak. Their wings are light gray and tipped in black.

Herring Gulls mate for life and raise their chicks together. They take turns incubating the eggs, feeding chicks, and protecting them from other gulls, birds, and animals who see chicks as food. Every day, Herring Gull parents bring as much as half a pound of food for each chick.

A GATHERING OF SHOREBIRDS

Sanderling

SANDERLING BY RAY HENNESSY/SHUTTERSTOCK

Listen

Sanderlings are one of the world's most widespread shorebirds. As you walk along the beach, you might see them running back and forth with the waves.

This brown and white "peep" (a nickname for a sandpiper) may look ordinary, but every summer it flies to the Arctic to breed, and in the winter, some fly as far south as Argentina!

Willet

WILLET BY STEVE BOWER/SHUTTERSTOCK

Listen

Willets are common on beaches, but you might not notice these brown-gray birds quietly probing the sand with their long bills. When they fly, you will see their bold wing pattern with a large white bar surrounded by black. Listen for their piercing calls. The tip of a Willet's bill is so sensitive, it doesn't need to see well to eat well. It can search for food even at night.

Snowy Egret

Snowy Egrets live near saltwater marshes, brackish pools (part saltwater, part freshwater), and freshwater lakes and rivers. The Snowy Egret is an elegant, medium sized heron with a long slender neck, black bill, black legs, and bright yellow feet. It stands over the water, stirring the bottom with its feet to bring up fish, frogs, worms, or crustaceans such as shrimp or crabs. Then it waits for just the right moment to spear a fish, or grab a crab with its sharply pointed bill.

During the breeding season, Snowy Egrets grow long, delicate plumes that catch the slightest breeze. These beautiful feathers once decorated women's hats, and were in such high demand that the birds were nearly hunted to extinction. Luckily, bird lovers spoke up, and The Migratory Bird Treaty Act was passed in 1918 to protect egrets. Since then, their populations have recovered.

SNOWY EGRET BY SVETLANA FOOTE/SHUTTERSTOCK

Listen

STARFISH OR SEA STAR?

For a long time, sea stars were called starfish, but they are not fish. They don't have scales, fins, or gills like fish do and are related to sea urchins and sand dollars.

Sea stars pump seawater into hundreds of tiny tube feet with suction cups so they can stick to rocks and move around under the waves. This is why it is very important for them to stay wet.

SEA STAR BY PICTUREPARTNERS/SHUTTERSTOCK

The way that sea stars eat is different from how we eat. When a sea star finds a clam, it wraps its arms around it so there is no escape. Then, with a powerful sucking action, it makes a small space between the shells and pushes its stomach into the clam to digest it. After it has eaten, it sucks its stomach back into its body!

BLUE-BLOODED HORSESHOE CRAB

Horseshoe crabs are not really "crabs." They are more closely related to spiders. Their sharp tail looks like a weapon, but it's used for steering in water and righting themselves in the sand. They have curious blue blood that is used by scientists to fight infection in human vaccines.

HORSESHOE CRAB BY JAROUS/SHUTTERSTOCK

Female horseshoe crabs will lay as many as 90,000 eggs at a time, but only 10 will become adults. Millions of migrating shorebirds from Central and South America eat the eggs in spring and early summer when they stop for a rest at Delaware and Chesapeake bays. The rich horseshoe crab eggs provide fuel for them to finish their journey to summer breeding grounds in the north.

A CAST OF CRABS

Crabs will eat just about anything: small snails, clams, insects, other crabs. They also get rid of "trash" on the beach by eating bits and pieces of dead animals and plants.

They have eyes that sit on top of stalks that they can pull in and out and move in a complete circle so they can see behind without having to turn around. Their gills allow them to breathe on the beach and under water. Like the sea star, if a leg is damaged or cut off, they will grow a new one.

Hermit Crab

HERMIT CRAB BY HAVESEEN/SHUTTERSTOCK

Despite being called hermits, they don't like to be alone and will hang out with 100 or more other hermit crabs. Unlike most crabs, the hermit crab's belly is not protected by its own hard shell, and it lives inside shells borrowed from snails and mollusks. Unfortunately, these shells don't grow with them and when they no longer fit, the crabs must search for a bigger shell. They put the larger shell in just the right position, and pop into their new home as quickly as possible to protect their soft abdomens.

Sometimes when hermit crabs need a larger shell, they line up on the sand from largest crab to smallest, and have a shell exchange. The biggest hermit crab will have a larger home ready and waiting, and as it pops inside it, one by one, the smaller crabs behind jump into the larger shells in front of them.

Jonah Crab

JONAH CRAB BY USFWS

It is easy to know when you see a Jonah crab because its shell is almost round and doesn't have the sharp points. Like birds, Jonah crabs migrate, but in the water. They move offshore in fall and winter, and inshore in spring and summer.

Fiddler Crab

FIDDLER CRAB BY CUSON/SHUTTERSTOCK

Fiddler crabs are closely related to ghost crabs. Their name comes from the way they feed. They hold their enormous claw (the fiddle) in front of their body while they use their smaller claw (the bow) to sift through the sand. As they bring food up to their mouth with the smaller claw, it looks like they are playing a fiddle.

HOW YOU CAN HELP OUR BEACHES AND WILDLIFE

~ Seabirds eat bits of plastic they think is food, and sometimes feed it to their chicks. The plastic gets stuck in the digestive system and can eventually kill them. Birds and other animals may also become entangled in fishing lines washed up on the beach. Help keep beaches beautiful and safe for wildlife by picking up trash. When you're at home, reuse or recycle plastics to keep them out of the ocean. Choose a reusable water bottle and bring reusable bags or boxes when you go shopping.

~ Don't let your dog chase after birds on the beach. Dogs love a good chase, but they can prevent birds from resting and eating. They may also destroy nests and eggs of birds that nest on the sand. During Piping Plover nesting season, many beaches are closed to dogs, so be sure to check your local beach for restrictions.

~ Save energy to help keep our planet healthy. As temperatures warm, the ice melts at the earth's poles, causing sea levels to rise. If this happens too much, the beaches we enjoy today could someday be under water. Do your part to reduce the use of energy by turning off the lights, TV, or computer when you're not using them. When you can, walk or ride your bicycle instead of riding in the car.

~ Visit *AllAboutBirds.org* to learn more about birds and the amazing things they do, and share what you learn with your family and friends.

TheCornellLab of Ornithology

The Cornell Lab of Ornithology is a leading voice
in the study, appreciation, and conservation of birds.
As with all Cornell Lab Publishing Group books,
35 percent of the net proceeds from the sale of
On Gull Beach will directly support the Cornell
Lab's projects such as children's educational
and community programs.